Uranus

Neptune

Pluto

Mercury

Sun

hrinking Violet

by Cari Best

Illustrated by Giselle Potter

MELANIE KROUPA BOOKS
FARRAR, STRAUS AND GIROUX · NEW YORK

For Alexandra—My Very Excellent Daughter
—C.B.

For Kieran
—G.P.

Text copyright © 2001 by Cari Best
Illustrations copyright © 2001 by Giselle Potter
All rights reserved
Distributed in Canada by Douglas & McIntyre Ltd.
Color separations by Banta Digital Group
Printed and bound in the United States of America by Worzalla
Book design by Jennifer Browne
First edition, 2001
1   3   5   7   9   10   8   6   4   2

Library of Congress Cataloging-in-Publication Data
Best, Cari.
   Shrinking Violet / by Cari Best ; illustrated by Giselle Potter.—1st ed.
   p. cm.
   Summary: Violet, who is very shy and hates for anyone to look at her in
school, finally comes out of her shell when she is cast as Lady Space in a
play about the solar system and saves the production from disaster.
   ISBN 0-374-36882-I
   [1. Bashfulness—Fiction. 2. Schools—Fiction. 3. Theater—Fiction.]
1. Potter, Giselle, ill. II. Title.

PZ7.B46575 Sh 2000
[E]—dc21

                                                    99-88966

On the afternoon of the annual Carry-the-Flag Day at school, Violet felt her stomach turn upside down. "I can't do it," she told her teacher, Mrs. Maxwell. "Everyone will be watching me."

"We will be watching your lovely maple-leaf flag," said Mrs. Maxwell, smiling.

"And how high you wave it," added her best friend, Opal.

"Not to mention your Flag Day smile," said Harriet.

"And how well you march to the music," offered John Philip.

"*I* will be watching your fat knees," said Irwin, smirking and wrinkling up his nose.

Violet's cheeks blushed rhubarb red. She passed her flag to Bernie and found a seat in the very last row. Everyone stared . . . which made Violet itch and scratch and twirl her hair. I wish I could just shrink away, she thought, pretending to tie her shoe.

In the meantime, a fine display of colored flags paraded across the room while Irwin, still smirking, wrote I MUST BE KIND TO OTHERS one hundred times, and Violet, still blushing, wrote I AM ALLERGIC TO ATTENTION on the inside of her hand.

"You don't really have fat knees," said Opal as she and Violet walked home after school.

"You have hairy arms!" said Irwin, bursting out of the bushes in front of Mrs. Hawthorne's house. All the neighbors stared . . . which made Violet itch and scratch and twirl her hair. I wish I could just shrink away, she thought, counting the number of hairs she had up and down her arms.

That afternoon in Violet's kitchen, Opal read Violet's palm.

"It says here that one day soon, you will do something about that Irwin," she said.

"You're not a very good reader," said Violet.

But Opal continued. "You'll tell him that he has dirty ears and flea-bitten fingernails."

Violet took a closer look. "And blue-cheese breath and llama lips," she added.

"And then I'll tell him he belongs in the zoo," she giggled.

"Now you're talking!" said Opal, hugging Violet.

But the thought of meeting up with Irwin face-to-face made Violet itch and scratch and twirl her hair.

"I can't do it," she said. "Everyone will be watching me."

For as long as Violet could remember, she didn't like to be watched. She never made waves in the swimming pool. Or swallowing sounds at snack time. She didn't sing in the Salute to Spring concert. And she wouldn't dance when someone asked her.

For as long as Violet could remember, *she* liked to do all the watching. She knew the fast swimmers from the slow ones. And exactly what everyone brought for snack. She knew the second someone sang off-key. And who always stepped on whose new shoes.

The more Violet looked and listened, the sharper she got. Violet showed Opal that a butterfly had six legs and four wings. And told her how crickets rub their wings together to chirp. Violet could rumble like a hungry stomach, and grumble like King Kong when he got angry. Opal was impressed.

Violet could do other things, too.
"My fellow Americans," she declared like the President.

She could sing the "Hound Dog" song like Elvis Presley,

shout "That ball is o v e r the fence!" like a sports announcer . . .

and hold up her torch like the Statue of Liberty.

But her favorite of all was reciting Captain Hook's walk-the-plank speech. "Yo ho ho!" she sneered, the end of a hanger sticking menacingly out of her sleeve.

Opal applauded wildly. "You're so good, Violet. Why don't you do your acting for show and tell?"

Violet stopped dead in her tracks. "I'd rather eat an ant," she said, squirming.

A few days later, Violet squirmed again. At school Mrs. Maxwell announced that the class would be putting on a play about the solar system. "Each of you will have a part," Mrs. Maxwell said, "like an asteroid or a meteoroid, a comet or a planet, a satellite or a star."

"What will Violet be?" asked Irwin, wrinkling up his nose. "Some deadly sewer gas?"

Violet covered her face with her astronomy book and itched and scratched and twirled her hair.

After lunch the parts were given out. Violet was relieved when she didn't hear her name. And then she did. "The role of Lady Space will be played by Violet," said Mrs. Maxwell.

When no one was looking, Violet told her teacher, "I can't do it."

So Mrs. Maxwell explained. "There will be nine planets, eight asteroids, seven meteoroids, six comets, and five stars onstage. But Lady Space will be speaking from a dark and mysterious place—offstage."

For once Violet didn't itch and Violet didn't scratch. She didn't twirl her hair and she didn't want to shrink away. She went home and learned her lines, bouncing her voice all around the house like an echo.

"You can't see me, but I'm here, all right. I'm everywhere. *I* am SPACE."

Violet practiced under the coats in the closet,

on top of the onions in the basement,

and in front of the toothbrushes in the bathroom. In no time at all, she knew her lines perfectly. And everyone else's, too.

Mrs. Maxwell's class rehearsed long and hard. "Louder," coached Mrs. Maxwell, until everyone got it just right—especially Violet, who had to say her part from way up in the projection booth.

Sometimes there were little problems, with costumes, or with scenery. But there was only one big problem. The nine planets kept forgetting where they were supposed to stand.

"Remember," Mrs. Maxwell said, "where you stand onstage depends on how far your planet is from the Sun." Then she taught them a funny phrase:

My   Very   Excellent   Mother   Just   Served   Us   Nine   Pizzas

MERCURY   VENUS   EARTH   MARS   JUPITER   SATURN   URANUS   NEPTUNE   PLUTO

But the planets were still all mixed up.

Just about everyone had the jitters on opening night. When the curtain went up, Lady Space was the first to speak. "Our solar system is part of a giant galaxy called the Milky Way," she said. "And the Sun, a star, is at the center."

Violet watched as Harriet, looking big and bright, stood in the middle while all the planets moved around her. "Ooooh," said the audience when Saturn whirled her rings.

Then, right on cue, the
spooky outer-space music
changed to standing-in-one-
place music. Everyone
remembered what to do.
Everyone except Irwin,
who was Mars.

Irwin kept moving.
Around and around like
the spin cycle on a
washing machine.

Into the scenery and over the props.

Tripping, ripping, bumping, and jumping.

Faster and faster . . .
spinning and
spinning . . .

until he was all spun out.

Now the planets looked like this:

My Very Excellent Pizza Just Served Us Nine Mothers
First Mercury started speaking. Then Venus. Then
Earth. Mars was next. But *where* was Irwin?

Suddenly Violet knew what she had to do. She put on her
Irwin-the-smirk face and in a perfect imitation she began:

"I am Irwin the Alien, maddest Martian on Mars.
Scientists think there is no intelligent life on my planet.
And they're right!"

The audience laughed as if it were all part of the play.

Violet continued. "The surface of Mars is as red as blood. That's why I'm named after the god of war. Anyone want to fight?"

This time the audience roared. Irwin scrambled to his feet, gave Pluto one last push, and finally took his proper place.

Everyone stared . . . which made Irwin fidget and burp and twiddle his thumbs.

After that it was smooth sailing. At the end of the play, there were three curtain calls. The spotlight looked for Violet. Until Opal said, "The beautiful and talented Lady Space wishes to remain dark and mysterious." Which made the audience clap again, and throw a storm of confetti.

While the cast was getting ready to go home, Violet had a lot of backstage visitors. One of them was Irwin. "Thanks," he whispered. "I would have looked so dumb."

Then when he saw that everyone was watching, he said out loud, "Maybe you don't have fat knees or hairy arms. And maybe you don't smell like sewer gas either. But you do have a really bad case of skeleton elbows." And Irwin smirked and wrinkled up his nose. Just like he always did.

Only this time, even though everyone was watching her, Violet didn't feel like shrinking away. She knew she had finally done something about that Irwin. In her own way. And this time, she didn't bother to check her elbows. She knew they were exactly the way they were supposed to be. Just like she was.